MÖLANG

Butterfly Chase

by Lana Crespin

SCHOLASTIC INC.

10 9 8 7 6 5 4 3 2 1   17 18 19 20 21

ISBN 978-1-338-22288-3

Printed in the U.S.A. 40

First printing 2017

Cover design by Becky James and
Interior design by Angela Jun

It is a bright and sunny day, and Molang and Piu Piu are having a picnic with their friends.

Suddenly a beautiful butterfly floats by their picnic blanket.

"Ooh," says Molang.

Molang and Piu Piu reach for their butterfly nets. They want to catch the butterfly and look at it up close.

But the butterfly doesn't want to be caught. Molang and Piu Piu catch each other instead!

They giggle as they chase the butterfly through the meadow.

Molang and Piu Piu find the butterfly fluttering in some tall weeds. This time, they are sure to catch it. They swing their nets. *Swoosh!*

Uh-oh. They've caught something, but it's not the butterfly. It's a cow!

"Moo," says the cow. It doesn't like being caught. It tosses them into a bush!

After some time, Molang and Piu Piu spot the butterfly resting on a wildflower. Piu Piu will dress up as a flower, so the butterfly will come to them.

But Piu Piu's costume is so good, even the cow thinks Piu Piu is a flower. Piu Piu doesn't want to be eaten and runs away! The cow is shocked to see a flower get up and run!

Molang and Piu Piu run into their friends. They all go tumbling down a hillside, right into a big patch of wildflowers.

There are butterflies all around them!
Butterflies love flowers because they drink
nectar from them—flowers are like a picnic just for
butterflies!

On their way home, Molang and Piu Piu pass by a beautiful garden. Molang has an idea! Molang and Piu Piu will plant their own flower garden. The butterflies will come to their garden to drink all the nectar from the flowers!

Molang and Piu Piu get to work. They rake and they shovel. They plow and they dig.

All the while, a group of birds watches them from a tree.

Finally, Molang and Piu Piu plant the seeds. With water and sunlight, the seeds will grow into flowers. Molang and Piu Piu leave the garden to fetch their watering cans.

But when they get back, the birds are busy eating all the seeds!

That pesky flock of birds ate every last seed!

Molang and Piu Piu plant more seeds.
This time they do not let the birds out of their sight.

They watch over their garden all day long. But as time passes, they get sleepier and sleepier until . . . "Zzzz," Molang snores. They are both fast asleep!

When the two friends wake up, they notice all of their seeds have been eaten by the birds. Again! What can they do to keep the birds away?

Molang builds a very scary scarecrow to frighten away the birds. But it is so scary, even Piu Piu is afraid of it.

Uh-oh! Now Molang is afraid of it, too!

Molang dresses the scarecrow in different
clothes, adds a straw hat and heart-shaped
glasses, and gives the scarecrow a new mouth.

"Ta-da!" Molang cries. Now the scarecrow looks
very nice.

But scarecrows are not meant to look nice. Scarecrows are meant to be scary.

The hungry birds aren't afraid of the scarecrow anymore. One even lands on its shoulder!

"Hmm." Molang and Piu Piu think. What if they feed the birds enough so that they aren't hungry anymore? Molang grabs some bowls and string. Piu Piu gets their extra seeds. Together, they turn the scarecrow into a bird feeder!

Molang and Piu Piu dance as they replant their seeds. Now they can feed everyone—the birds can eat some of the seeds, and the rest of the seeds will grow into flowers to feed the butterflies! What a great day for everyone!